Duffy and the Devil

A Cornish tale retold by

HARVE ZEMACH

Duffy and the Devil

with pictures by

MARGOT ZEMACH

A Sunburst Book
Farrar, Straus and Giroux

For Elizabeth and Benjamin

Copyright © 1973 by Farrar, Straus and Giroux, Inc.
All rights reserved
Library of Congress catalog card number: 72-81491
Distributed in Canada by Douglas & McIntyre Ltd.
First edition, 1973
Sunburst edition, 1986
Printed in June 2010 in China by South China Printing Co. Ltd.,
Dongguan City, Guangdong Province
9   11   13   15   14   12   10

ISBN: 978-0-374-41897-7 (pbk.)

Squire Lovel of Trove had no wife. His housekeeper, Old Jone, did the cooking and the cleaning for him. But the sharpness had long since gone out of her eyesight, so she couldn't do fine chores any more, like spinning and sewing and knitting. After a time the squire's clothes got so rough and ragged that he thought he'd better go find a maid to be Jone's helper.

With that in mind he rode up to Buryan Churchtown one fine morning.

On his way into the town, he suddenly heard an awful screeching and hollering. The door of a cottage flew open and out ran a blubbering, bawling girl chased by an old woman who was clouting her with a broom and shouting, "You lazy bufflehead, you!"

"What's all this about, auntie?" cried the squire. "What's the cause of this confloption with you and Duffy?"

"Oh, your honor!" wailed the old woman. "What am I to do with this gashly girl? She gallivants with the boys all day long and never stops at home to boil the porridge, nor knit the stockings, nor spin the yarn!"

"Don't believe a word she says, your honor," spoke up the girl, dabbing at her teary eyes with a corner of her dusty apron. "I do all the work, I spin like a saint, I knit like an angel, and all I get for it is clouts and clumps."

Squire Lovel could see that Duffy and the woman would be glad to get quits of one another, so he asked the girl how would she like to come to Trove Manor to help his old housekeeper with the work that needed sharp eyes and quick fingers.

"Try me, your honor," answered Duffy. "You'll not be sorry, I promise you that."

"Good riddance to bad rummage!" muttered the old woman. Duffy bunched up her skirts, scrambled onto the squire's horse, sat herself ladylike behind him, and they jogged off down to Trove.

When they got there, old Jone met them at the door. "This is Duffy," said Squire Lovel, "who is come down to help you knit and spin. Give her some dinner, Joney dear, and show her what to do."

Duffy ate her fill, and she and the housekeeper got acquainted, and pretty soon Jone led her upstairs to the loft where the wool was kept and the spinning done. First thing, Jone said, was the squire needed a new pair of stockings—the ones he was wearing had been patched to pieces. She set a chair by the spinning wheel, took down some wool that had already been carded and only needed spinning into yarn, and stood by to watch her new helper work.

"It's right strange," said Duffy, "but all my life I never have been able to do a stitch of work with anybody watching me. 'Specially spinning. For that, I just have to be alone by myself."

So Jone left Duffy alone, and it was good she did, because the fact is Duffy didn't know a thing about spinning. She tried to figure out how the spinning wheel worked, and pretty soon she had it apart, and the parts rolling around on the floor, and herself and the machine and the wool in a terrible tangle.

"Curse the spinning!" she cried. "And the knitting, too! The devil can make Squire Lovel's stockings for all I care!"

No sooner said than out from behind a stack of fleeces appeared an oogly little squinny-eyed creature with a long tail. "At your service, Duffy my dear," said the devil with a bow. "I'll do the spinning for you, and the knitting, too. How'd you like that?"

"Are you sure you know how to work all these little whilly-gogs and whizamagees, mister?" asked Duffy.

"Simple as pudding," replied the devil. He sat down at the spinning wheel, and with his fingers flying so fast that Duffy couldn't even see them, he had the whole batch of wool spun into yarn in a couple of blinks.

"Stockings, did you say?" said he, pulling some knitting needles out of his pocket. Clickety-clickety-clack and instead of the yarn there was a pair of stockings. "I believe they'll fit the squire very nicely," he said.

"How much do I have to pay you?" asked Duffy.

"Not a penny," replied the devil. "Listen: I'll knit and I'll spin as much as you like—to me it's just a game. But at the end of three years *I'll take you away*—unless you can tell me my name!"

"Your name?" said Duffy.

"That's right. Unless you can tell me my name—or my daddy's name, either will do, they're both the same! You have three whole years to guess what it is. You get as many guesses as you please. And meanwhile, all the spinning and knitting gets done without your lifting a finger. Think it over." And suddenly as he had come, he disappeared.

Duffy spent the afternoon snoozing pleasantly up in the loft, and at suppertime skipped downstairs with the stockings draped over her arm. Old Jone was amazed at the speed, and when she felt the stockings, exclaimed, "Why, they're soft as silk!"

"And they're strong as leather!" declared the squire next day. He had put on his new stockings to go out hunting, and after long hours of trudging through furze and brambles and plodging through brake and briar, his stockings and his legs came home entirely dry and without a scratch. "Never have there been such stockings!" he declared.

The day after that was Sunday, and Squire Lovel wore his stockings to church. Neighbors and acquaintances kept him standing outside admiring the pattern and the fit and the silky softness and the leatherlike toughness of his stockings until the parson wondered what all the fuss was about. And when he, too, had seen the squire's stockings, he said: "That Duffy! She can spin like a saint and knit like an angel!"

Well, pretty soon Squire Lovel was eager to have Duffy make him some more things. A hunting jacket out of good solid home-spun, for example—wouldn't that be something! He told Duffy what he wanted, and she took herself upstairs to the loft.

There was that grinning devil, sitting at the spinning wheel, waiting for her. "The stockings seem to have been a success, Duffy dear," he said. "The whole neighborhood is talking about them."

"Oh, yes," replied Duffy, "but now Squire wants a jacket, and who knows what it'll be next."

"No trouble at all, Duffy," said the squinny-eyed one. "But what about our bargain?"

So Duffy shrugged her shoulders and did her deal with the devil—three years of that knitting and spinning of his, and then he could take her away if he wanted to. The hunting jacket was made, and in the days and weeks after that, Duffy fetched many a fine article of cloth and clothing down from the loft. Once in a while she tried guessing some names, but they were all wrong, and finally she just put it out of mind. Squire Lovel was more pleased with her all the time, and she was enjoying the easy life.

One day Squire Lovel thought to himself: wouldn't Duffy make a fine wife for somebody, the way she spins and knits? Wouldn't she make a fine wife for *me?* So he asked her to marry him, and they had a dandy wedding, and before you know it, Duffy wasn't just plain Duffy any more, but Lady Duffy Lovel of Trove! And she was wearing satin gowns, and the best of silks and laces, and red-heeled shoes from France. Those were her dancing shoes, and whenever she wasn't up in the loft pretending to be knitting something new for the squire, she could be found on the green by the mill, dancing with the other ladies of the neighborhood, frolicking away the time while the corn was grinding.

But it couldn't last forever. Three years is what the devil said, and when three years were almost up, he started jibing and jeering at her, grinning and winking and behaving all cock-a-hoop, and she soon remembered what he said about taking her away unless she could tell him his name. That set her grieving over her troubles.

Old Jone noticed how glumpy and gloomy Duffy was acting, and she wasn't surprised when one day, all in tears, Duffy told her the whole story.

"So *that's* how come!" said Jone. "Well, when you're in the world as many years as I've been, you learn all sorts of secrets—even some the devil hasn't heard about. I'll do my best to help you, Duffy." She said she'd need a keg of the strongest beer out of the cellar, and told Duffy not to go to bed that night until the squire got home from hunting, no matter how late.

Squire Lovel went out hunting as usual that day, and though he tramped over the moors until he and his dogs were drooping tired and hungry, he couldn't catch a thing. Nightfall found him down by Lamorna. He had just about decided to go home empty-handed, when up started a hare—as fine a hare as ever was seen. The dogs gave chase, the squire followed close behind, and on they went through water and mud, a mile or more. Then just when he thought he had the hare cornered, it bounded down a hole that was the entrance to a cavern underground—known to all in the neighborhood as the fuggy-hole, where witches were said to have their midnight meetings.

The dogs stopped in their tracks, howling and jowling, terrified to follow any farther. But Squire Lovel plunged right in, the owls and the bats flapping round his head. At the very end of the cavern he saw a glimmering fire, and about it the witches were gathering. Some were riding on ragwort, some on brooms, some were floating on their three-legged stools, and some astride giant leeks. Tending the fire was an old woman, and Squire Lovel thought she looked just like his housekeeper, Jone. And in the midst of them all was a queer little squinny-eyed creature with a long tail that he held up high in the air and twirled.

The one that looked like Jone gave the creature with the tail a swig of beer from time to time. Between times she scratched a tune on a fiddle, and the creature and the witches danced round the fire, faster and faster, swirling like the wind.

The squire watched it all gawk-eyed, until at last a feeling came over him of wanting to get in on the frolic. So he swung up his hat and his hunting staff, and let out a whoop: "Go to it, old devil, and witches all!"

Zam! Up flashed the fire, all went black, and the next thing he knew he was racing like a hound, with all the witches at his heels, and he didn't stop until he got to the safe side of the horseshoe on his own front door.

Duffy was still waiting up for him. Her forehead was wrinkled with worry. Squire Lovel flopped into his armchair in front of the fire, and as soon as he had his breath back, he told her what had happened.

"Are you sure that's everything?" she said when he had finished telling it. "Wasn't there anything else?"

"Why, yes! Come to think of it," said the squire, "there was a song that the devil-creature sang after taking one last swig of the beer."

"How did it go?" begged Duffy.

The squire searched his mind. "I think it went like this:

"Tomorrow! Tomorrow! Tomorrow's the day!
I'll take her! I'll take her! I'll take her away!
Let her weep, let her cry, let her beg, let her pray—
She'll never guess my name is . . ."

"Is what?" cried Duffy.

". . . is . . . ah, I think it starts with a T . . . that's it, Tarraway!
She'll never guess my name is Tarraway!"

Then Duffy laughed and laughed, and her laughing made the
squire laugh, and when they had both laughed until they couldn't
laugh any more, they went to bed.

The next day when the devil appeared up in the loft, Duffy was waiting for *him*.

"Time's up, Duffy dear," he said. His eyes weren't squinny now—they were goggly. And his tail was twitching.

"What about guessing your name?" said Duffy.

"Of course! One last guess—then you're mine!" replied the devil. He held up his tail and twirled it over his head.

"Tarraway!" cried Duffy. "Tarraway, Tarraway!"

The devil howled with disappointment. "That was no guess! You were told!" He stamped his foot. "You were *told!*" He stamped his foot again. "You were TOLD!" He stamped his foot a third time, and as he did, there was a flash of flame and a puff of smoke, and he was gone. And at that same moment all the devil's knitting turned to ashes.

Squire Lovel was out on the moors when it happened. The day was cold and the wind piercing. Suddenly the stockings dropped from his legs and the homespun from his back. He had to come home with nothing on but his hat and his shoes.

And when he got home, there was old Jone sweeping up little piles of ashes all around the house, and Duffy following after her, exclaiming loudly: "All my work! Gone up in smoke! I swear I'll never knit another thing ever again!"

And she never did.